ABB CHA

Chaucer, G.
The

D1189818

P

Penguin 🐧 Readers

MAR - - 2023

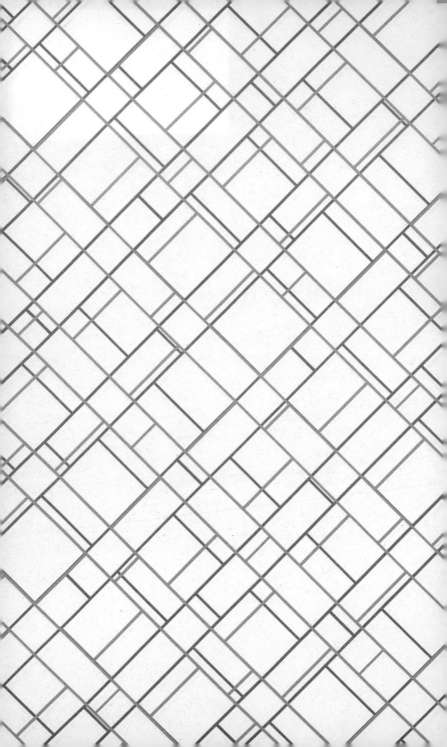

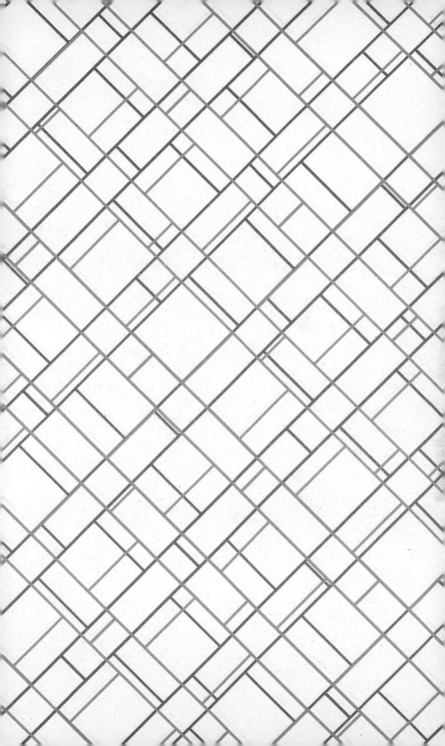

Penguin Readers

THE KNIGHT'S TALE

GEOFFREY CHAUCER

LEVEL

S

RETOLD BY ELIZABETH DOWSETT
ILLUSTRATED BY DYNAMO LTD
SERIES EDITOR: SORREL PITTS

ST. THOMAS PUBLIC LIBRARY

PENGUIN BOOKS

UK | USA | Canada | Ireland | Australia
India | New Zealand | South Africa

Penguin Books is part of the Penguin Random House group of companies
whose addresses can be found at global.penguinrandomhouse.com.
www.penguin.co.uk www.puffin.co.uk www.ladybird.co.uk

Penguin Readers edition of *The Knight's Tale* published by Penguin Books Ltd, 2021
001

Original text written by Geoffrey Chaucer
Text for Penguin Readers edition adapted by Elizabeth Dowsett
Text for Penguin Readers edition copyright © Penguin Books Ltd, 2021
Illustrated by Dynamo Ltd
Illustrations copyright © Penguin Books Ltd, 2021
Cover image copyright © Bolyuk Studio/Shutterstock

Printed and bound in Great Britain by Clays Ltd, Elcograf S.p.A.

The authorized representative in the EEA is Penguin Random House Ireland,
Morrison Chambers, 32 Nassau Street, Dublin D02 YH68

A CIP catalogue record for this book is available from the British Library

ISBN: 978-0-241-52082-6

All correspondence to:
Penguin Books
Penguin Random House Children's
One Embassy Gardens, 8 Viaduct Gardens,
London SW11 7BW

MIX
Paper from
responsible sources
FSC
www.fsc.org   FSC® C018179

Penguin Random House is committed to a
sustainable future for our business, our readers
and our planet. This book is made from Forest
Stewardship Council® certified paper.

Contents

People in the story

Arcita

Palamon

Theseus

Emily

The Story Teller

Venus
goddess of husbands and wives

Mars
god of knights

Diana
goddess of women

Saturn
Venus' father

New words

enemies

fight

free

god and goddess

king

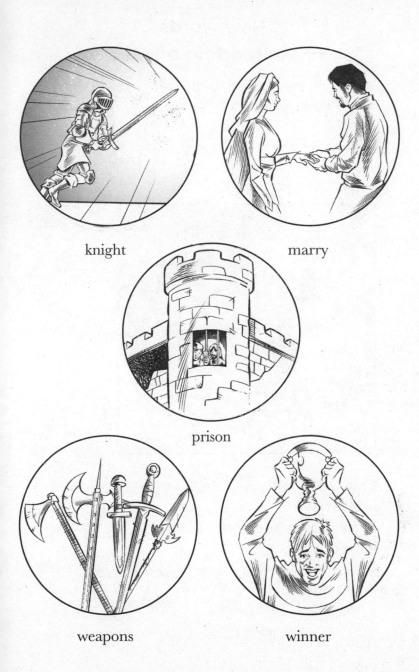

knight

marry

prison

weapons

winner

11

Before-reading questions

1 Look at the cover of this book. What do you think the story is about?

2 Chaucer is English, but the people in the story are in Greece 2,000 years before Chaucer. What do you know about Greece in these years?

3 Look at the "New words" on pages 10–11 and write the correct words in your notebook.

  a This person fights a lot. ....*knight*..........

  b People fight with these.

  c This person does not like you and you do not like them.

  d Bad people are here. They cannot go from here.

  e Two people do this. Now they are husband and wife.

  f People listen to this person.

4 Look at this picture. These people are knights. Write about
them in your notebook. Who are they? What do they do?
Are they young or old? Are they happy or sad?

THE KNIGHT'S TALE

Theseus is a **king** from Athens.
He **fights** many **enemies**.

Today, Thebes is mine!

One day, Emily is walking in the garden near the prison.

Emily's sister is Theseus's wife. Emily lives in Theseus's house.

One day, Theseus's old friend, Perotheus, comes to Athens.

Theseus, you are my friend. And Arcita is my friend. Please make him **free**.

24

Palamon is in prison.

But he can see Emily every day.

Arcita does good work for seven years.
Now he works with the king.

You're a good man, Philostrate.

36

42

44

45

46

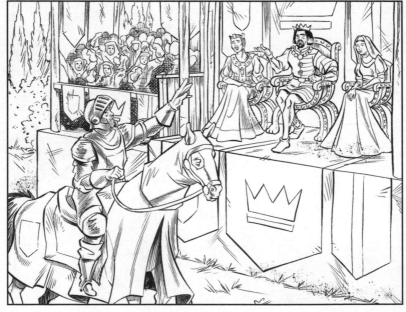

48

49

During-reading questions

1 How old is the story?
2 Who is Theseus?
3 Where do Theseus's men take Arcita and Palamon?
4 How are Arcita and Palamon in the same family?

1 Where does Emily live?
2 Perotheus says to Theseus, "Please make Arcita free."
  Why does he say this?
3 What is Arcita's new name?
4 How many years does Philostrate work in Theseus's house?

1 Who can marry Emily?
2 How many knights do Arcita and Palamon find?
3 When do Arcita and Palamon's knights come to Athens?
4 Who is Venus?

1 What does Emily want to be?
2 Who does Arcita ask for help?
3 Why are Palamon and Emily sad?
4 Who are now husband and wife?

After-reading questions

1 This story is called "The Knight's Tale". Why is this, do you think?

2 What does Theseus do to his enemies? (Pages 19 and 38)

3 Arcita says, "Is she a goddess?" Why does he say this about Emily? (Page 22)

4 Why are Arcita and Palamon enemies?

5 Arcita is free, but he is not happy. Why? (Page 26)

6 Palamon can see Emily every day, but he is not happy. Why? (Page 27)

7 Why can't Arcita sleep? (Page 28)

8 Theseus says, "You're a good man, Philostrate." Why does he say this? (Page 31)

9 Palamon wants to fight, but Arcita says, "Wait!" Why does he say this? (Page 33)

10 Why do Palamon, Emily and Arcita talk to the gods and goddesses?

11 Palamon says, "Kill us!" Why does he say this, do you think? (Page 38)

12 Which man is a good husband for Emily, do you think?

13 Is Theseus a good king, do you think?

14 Is it a happy story, do you think?

15 Are the gods and goddesses in the story good or bad, do you think?

Exercises

1 **Match the person to the words in your notebook.**
Example: 1 – b

1	Theseus	**a**	helps Palamon.
2	Arcita	**b**	is a king from Athens.
3	Palamon	**c**	marries Emily.
4	Emily	**d**	cannot stay in Athens.
5	Perotheus	**e**	is very beautiful.
6	Saturn	**f**	are happy.
7	The people of Athens	**g**	is Theseus's old friend.

2 **Complete these sentences in your notebook, using the *present continuous.***

1 Emily ......*is walking*....... in the garden near the prison. (**walk**)

2 "I .... to Athens. I can see Emily there!" (**go**)

3 "He ...." (**sleep**)

4 "Why .... you ....?" (**fight**)

5 "Father, Mars .... Arcita." (**help**)

3 **Write the correct answer in your notebook.**

Example: 1 – c

1 Knight 1:   These weapons are mine now!

Knight 2:   **a** No, they're not mine!

b But I want new weapons!

c And I want this money!

2 Palamon: She's mine.

Arcita: **a** Yes, she's yours!

b No, she's mine!

c She can be ours.

3 Palamon: You're my enemy!

Arcita: **a** And you're *my* enemy!

b And you're *my* friend!

c And you're not my friend!

4 Arcita: Do you have work for me?

Man at the door: **a** There's lots of work here.

b There's no work here.

c Please do my work for me.

5 Emily: How can I be a good wife?

Diana: **a** I can help you.

b You can't be a good wife.

c Marry the winner.

6 Venus: Father, Mars's knight is the winner. Help me!

Saturn: **a** Yes, I can help you, my child.

b No, I can't help you, my child.

c Wait, my child.

4 Put these sentences in the correct order in your notebook.

a .... Arcita and Palamon see Emily in the garden.

b .... Palamon and Emily are husband and wife.

c .... All of Athens is happy.

d ...*1*... Arcita and Palamon go to prison.

e .... All of Athens is sad.

f .... Arcita is free, but he cannot stay in Athens.

g .... Arcita is the winner.

h .... Saturn helps Venus's knight.

5 Complete these sentences in your notebook, using the verbs from the box.

fight	marry	kill	take	wait	look
	come		bring	help	

1 "..........*Take*.......... these men to Athens."

2 ".......... at that beautiful woman. I love her!"

3 ".......... Arcita here."

4 "We're enemies. .... me!"

5 ".......... ! We don't have weapons."

6 ".......... here on Saturday."

7 "We're bad knights. .... us!"

8 "Please .... my knight, Palamon."

9 "Emily, I love you. But Palamon is a good man. .... him."

6 Contract the words in bold in your notebook.

1 **It is** about two knights, Arcita and Palamon.
It's about two knights, Arcita and Palamon.

2 "**They are** our enemies."

3 "I **do not** know, Arcita."

4 "Our mothers are sisters. **We are** family."

5 "**There is** lots of work here."

6 "**You are** a good man, Philostrate."

7 "**I am** free!"

8 "Emily **cannot** marry two men."

7 Complete these sentences in your notebook, using the adjectives from the box.

beautiful	old	many	good	sad
	free	happy	new	

1 This is a very ......*old*...... story – a tale.

2 Theseus is a king from Athens. He fights .... enemies.

3 "Look at that .... woman. I love her!"

4 Arcita is ...., but he cannot stay in Athens.

5 "I have a .... name. It's Philostrate."

6 Arcita does .... work for seven years.

7 "Palamon and Emily, you're .... about Arcita. But now you're husband and wife."

8 The people of Athens are ....

8 Complete these sentences in your notebook, using the words from the box.

fight	prison	king	winner	free
	weapons		enemy	

1 Palamon is in ...._prison_........., but he can see Emily every day.
2 "I'm ...., but I can't eat or drink."
3 "I'm Arcita. I'm your ...."
4 "Be a good ....! Help them!"
5 "You can .... for her."
6 "The .... marries Emily."
7 "Get .... for your knights."

Project work

1 You are Palamon. You are in prison. Arcita is free. Write a letter to your family in Thebes.

2 You are talking to the goddess Venus. What does she think about the story? Write your questions for Venus and write her answers.

3 Learn more about Geoffrey Chaucer. Write questions and ask a friend about him.

4 Write a new end to the story. Who is the winner? Who marries? The story can be happy or sad.

5 Choose a person from the story. Make a poster of this person's social media page (Twitter, Instagram, etc.). Talk about your poster with a friend.

Arcita
@IloveEmily

252 posts   1.4k followers   145 following

Come to Athens, family and friends!
I'm fighting Palamon on Saturday. Come and watch!
The winner marries Emily.
3.45pm - 5 Jan xxxx
♥ 310 ☺76

Theseus @kingofAthens
The people of Athens are waiting . . .
3.48pm - 5 Jan xxxx

Palamon @winnerknight
Emily is mine!
3.50pm - 5 Jan xxxx

An answer key for all questions and exercises can be found at
www.penguinreaders.co.uk

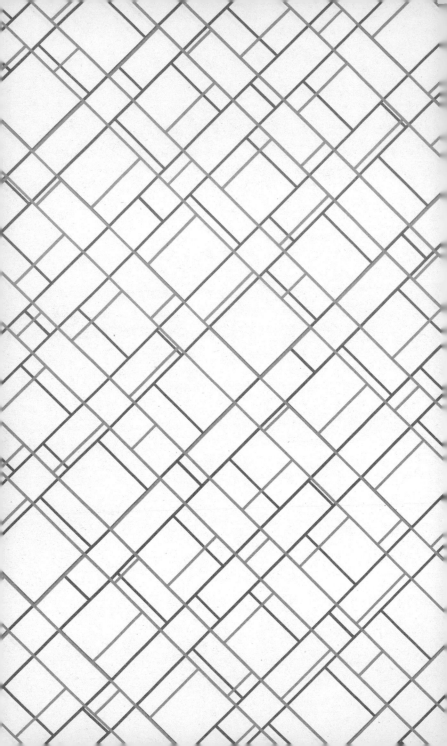

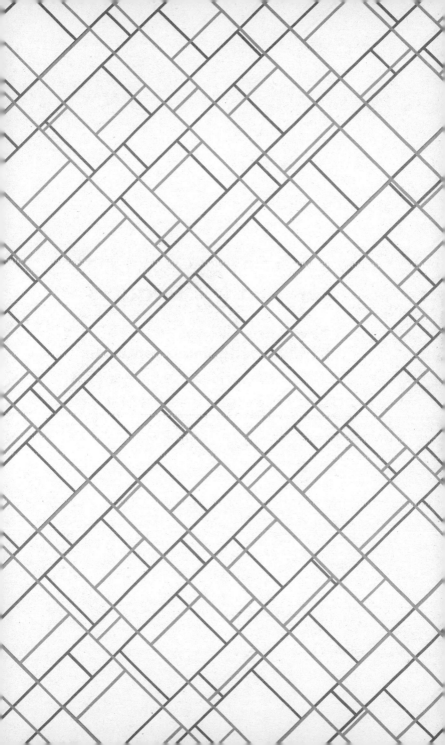

Penguin Readers

Visit **www.penguinreaders.co.uk**
for FREE Penguin Readers resources
and digital and audio versions of this book.